Henry and Mudge and a Very Merry Christmas

The Twenty-Fifth Book of Their Adventures

Story by Cynthia Rylant

Pictures by Suçie Stevenson

SCHOLASTIC INC.

New York   Toronto   London   Auckland   Sydney
Mexico City   New Delhi   Hong Kong   Buenos Aires

THE HENRY AND MUDGE BOOKS

ISBN 0-590-04080-4

12 11 10 9 8 7 6 5 4 3 2 1   5 6 7 8 9/0

Printed in the U.S.A.   23

First Scholastic printing, November 2005

READY-TO-READ is a registered trademark of Simon & Schuster, Inc.

Book design by Lucy Ruth Cummins

The text for this book is set in 18-point Goudy.

The illustrations are rendered in pen-and-ink and watercolor.

Contents

Christmastime

Henry and Henry's big dog, Mudge,
loved Christmastime.
They loved the smells—cinnamon in the
kitchen, peppermint in the living room,
pine on the front door.

5

But the smell they loved most of all was the
smell of cutout cookies.

This Christmas Henry's mother was making
cutout cookies for all of the relatives: for Henry's
grandmother and for Great-Grandpa Bill.

For Aunt Sally and for Uncle Jake.

For Cousin Annie and for Uncle Ed.

The relatives were coming for Christmas
breakfast, and they would all have cookies to
take home.

7

Henry and Mudge went into the kitchen
to help.

Henry cut out birds for his grandmother and
houses for Great-Grandpa Bill.

He cut out hearts for Aunt Sally and trucks for Uncle Jake.

He cut out bunnies for Annie and books for Uncle Ed.

Mudge just licked the floor a lot.
"Mudge is a good helper," Henry told
his mother.
"He's licking the kitchen all clean."

"Hmmm," said Henry's mother with a smile.
"Maybe we should make Christmas cookies
in **your** room!"

11

Applause

On Christmas Eve, Henry was very happy.

There were presents under the tree.

Snow was falling.

Candles were glowing.

13

"I think we should go caroling," said
Henry's father.
"With Annie and Uncle Ed."
"Great idea!" said Henry.

Annie and Uncle Ed came over from next door.
Annie was wearing big white earmuffs and
carrying her white bunny, Snowball.

"It looks like you have bunnies on your head,"
said Henry.
Annie giggled.

Mudge sniffed Snowball.
Then Mudge sniffed the earmuffs just to
make sure.

18

"It's too cold to take Snowball," Annie said.
"I'll just let her play in your room."
(Snowball loved Henry's room. There were so
many piles of things to hide under.)
Annie put Snowball in Henry's room.

Then Henry and Mudge and Henry's parents
and Annie and Uncle Ed all went caroling.
It was fun.

21

They got cookies and hot chocolate
and applause.
They even got an old shoe.

When they went back to Henry's house,
they lit candles and ate gingerbread and talked.

Snowball rode around the room on
Mudge's back.

Christmas was very near, and everyone was happy.

The Best Present

On Christmas morning, Annie and Uncle Ed
came over to open presents with Henry's family.

Annie got some new dresses and new lace hankies and new teacups for her collection. Henry got games and comics and two new fish (in his stocking!).

Mudge got a stuffed reindeer, and Snowball
got a coat.
"She's so **cute**!" said Annie.

Soon all of the relatives arrived for breakfast:
Grandma and Great-Grandpa Bill.
Aunt Sally.
Uncle Jake.
And the smell of pancakes filled the house.

Mudge and Snowball sat under the table while everyone ate.

A **lot** of food fell under the table.

Uncle Jake lost one whole pancake.
"Oops!" he said.

Aunt Sally lost one whole muffin.
"Oops!" she said.

Henry's father lost three slices of ham.
"Oops!" he said.

Mudge was very happy.

After breakfast the relatives went home with their Christmas cookies.

Great-Grandpa Bill was biting off a chimney on the way out the door.

When the house was quiet again, Henry helped his parents clean up the kitchen.
(Mudge helped too, of course.)

Then they all went out for a walk.
They left seed bells in the trees for the birds.

They left walnuts on the ground for the squirrels.

They left cracked corn for the deer.

When they got back home, Henry put his arm around Mudge.

"Merry Christmas, Mudge," Henry said.

"You're still the best present of all."

Mudge wagged and wagged and wagged.